3-6 cop 3

J   Wojciechowska, Maia, pseud.
            Hey, what's wrong with this one? Pictures
        by Joan Sandin.   New York, Harper & Row
        [1969]
            72 p. illus. 24cm.

Books by Maia Wojciechowska

"Hey, What's Wrong
With This One?"

"Hey, What's Wrong With This One?"

by Maia Wojciechowska, *pseud.*

Pictures by Joan Sandin

J

cop. 3 ✓

Harper & Row, Publishers

New York, Evanston, and London

697071727387654321

for Patrick, Peter, Vincent,
and their father,
with love and no regrets

How it began...

*D*uring the day it was not so bad. But at night, just before falling asleep, in the dark of their room, all three missed their mother very much.

They didn't talk about it, but each, in his own bed, thought about her. And each remembered her in his own way. Some of the memories had to do with all of them, with the family. But most were private. Each remembered best what she had meant just to him.

To the youngest of the three, to Mott, she was more a feeling than a person. For he had felt while she was alive that everything was right and nothing important could go wrong. It was as if by her mere presence she was able to make him happy and safe. Safe from all harm. When she was no longer with them, he felt a great, dangerous quiet inside and tried to shut it out by screaming when he talked. And Mott talked a lot. And his loud voice made everyone mad, especially his brothers. What no one knew was that the loudness of his voice made Mott mad too. What made him madder still was that there was nothing he could do about it. Instead of getting better, his voice got louder all the time. By the time he was seven years old, he hardly ever talked without shouting.

To Davidson, who was two years older than Mott, she had meant someone who noticed whenever he was being good. And when she was around, being good was not hard. Actually, being good gave him pleasure. Or maybe what gave him pleasure was seeing her pleased. What he loved best about her was her smile, which started in her eyes and seemed to fill the whole house. And just seeing her, the first thing in the morning and the last thing at night, made up for the fact that he had many problems, and the worst of them were his two brothers.

To Harley she had been the only person in the whole world who understood how it was with the firstborn. She seemed to have known, without being told by him, that life was tougher for him than for his brothers. Being oldest was no fun; it was a great responsibility. It made him mean sometimes, and worried most of the time. Yet she never noticed the meanness in him and tried to take the worries away. And above all else she loved him best. Of that he had always been sure.

During the first year after she died they remembered how she had looked and what she had said to them. Later they thought more about just the lack of her. And after two years they began to think about how it would be if they had another. And sometimes they talked about that.

"I hope she'd like flowers," Davidson said one night. "I would bring her flowers every day."

"Not in winter, stupid!" Harley said. "Flowers don't grow in winter!" He was angry, remembering how Davidson used to bring flowers to their mother and how he had wanted to but always forgot. "Besides," he screamed, "flowers fall apart, and she'd have to clean up after them."

"If she liked flowers she wouldn't mind," Davidson said, not screaming back, just enjoying Harley's anger. "And besides, I would help her clean up anyway. Like I used to help Mom." He was going to remind Harley of other things he used to do for her. But he didn't have a chance. Mott was screaming now:

"Hey, do you think she'd like things like beads and jewels and junk like that? Do you think we could get one who'd like lots of bright colors and fancy things on her hats and . . ."

"Cut it out," Harley yelled. "Who do you think you're talking about? Some kind of a freak or something? What she'd wear wouldn't matter! We need someone who'd understand things . . ."

What he really meant was that he wanted a mother

who would understand him and help him. But he didn't say that. He didn't want his brothers to know that he needed understanding or help.

"Hey, do you think she'd beat us?" Mott asked. He tried not to sound so loud, but his voice wouldn't be pushed around by him. It came out like a bullhorn.

"Of course she wouldn't beat us!" Harley yelled. "Dad wouldn't marry someone who'd beat us!"

"Maybe," Davidson said thoughtfully, "Dad wouldn't know about it. Maybe she'd be nice around him, but maybe she'd beat us when he wasn't home."

"She wouldn't beat us!" Harley shouted. "Dad would know that much about her."

"Maybe," Davidson said, "she'd yell at us a lot."

"Hey, I wouldn't even care if she beat us a little," Mott said. "And I wouldn't care if she yelled at us a lot. She could yell at us all day long if she was nice."

"If she was nice, jackass, she wouldn't yell at all!" Harley shouted. And then, because they made him so very mad, he hit both of them—each with one hand.

Their father had named them after a Harley-Davidson motorcycle he had loved once when he was a very young man. The four of them lived in a small town not too far from New York City. Each of the boys had a pony. They shared a sheep dog and a Siamese cat who was mortally afraid of noise and spent all his time hiding under the living-room sofa. The boys had all sorts of toys, and two television sets, and bikes. The only thing they did not have was a mother.

"Hey, Dad," Mott shouted at his father at the breakfast table one day, "why don't you get us a mother?"

"You just don't go out and get mothers!" Harley said, ramming his elbow into Mott's ribs.

"Why not, Dad?" Davidson asked, looking at his father, who was trying to read the morning paper. "It couldn't be that hard. Why can't you, Dad? Why can't you get us a mother?"

"Hey, I asked first!" Mott shouted.

Their father tried to ignore them. But it never seemed to do any good. He knew they would go on until they got an answer.

"How about it, Dad?" Davidson asked again.

"Hey, how about it, Dad?" Mott chimed in.

Harley tried to kick them both under the table, but they knew he would, so they moved their legs out of the way. Harley's face got very red.

Mott and Davidson watched Harley. They loved to see him get mad. When he did, he gritted his teeth. They waited for him to do it now. And when he did, they burst out laughing. Harley raised his fists to hit them, but just then their father spoke:

"Do you three seriously think," he said and looked at each in turn, "that there is a woman in her right mind who'd want to live in this house? With you three fighting all the time? Do you think any woman could stand seeing what you do to your room? How you throw things around? And how you get holes in your pants all the time? And how about the ponies? Do you clean after them? Do you ever feed them on time? And how about the dog and the cat? And the bikes you leave in the driveway each day? Do you really think that anyone would want to live here with us?"

"There might be someone," Davidson said, "who wouldn't mind. And besides, we'd change."

"We'd be very good. All the time," Mott yelled. "If we had a mother, we'd watch ourselves."

Harley wasn't going to say anything. But the temptation to put in his two cents was too great.

"It would be different," he said. "If we had a mother, I'd make sure *they* were good."

"Hey, what will she be like?" Mott wanted to know. As far as he was concerned everything was settled now. They all agreed to be good. And there was no point in waiting. "Will you get us a pretty one or an ugly one? Make sure she doesn't have warts. I wouldn't want one that's too skinny, but I'd rather have a really skinny one than a fat one. And . . ."

"Will you three cut it out?" their father said, very loudly this time.

"I didn't say anything," Harley pointed out.

He didn't like the way his father always seemed to confuse him with his brothers. He was not like them. But his father didn't understand this, and he included Harley in everything they got blamed for. If they were to get a new mother, Harley thought now, she would have to be like the one they used to have. She would have to *know* that he was different. If she couldn't understand that much, he wouldn't want her around.

"Hey, let's clean our room up!" Mott yelled, jumping up from his chair and upsetting his cereal bowl. He was out of the door before his father noticed the cereal dribbling down to the floor.

"Mott, come back here!" his father shouted after him.

Mott came right back. He knew what his father wanted, but he decided to act as if he didn't.

"What else do you want me to do, Dad?" he asked and smiled at his father. "If you'd get her today I could . . ."

"I want you to clean up this mess," his father said, pointing to the spilled cereal. "And I want all three of you to shape up. There will be some new rules around here. From now on the housekeeper doesn't go inside your room. The three of you will have to cope as best as you can. And I will inspect it each day when I get home from work. It better be clean. And you"—he turned to Mott—"just look at your face! I want you to wipe your face right after you put anything in your mouth."

"Even before swallowing?" Mott shouted.

"If you've got a moustache before you swallow, yes."

"I'll starve to death!" Mott protested.

"Harley, when was the last time you shined your shoes?" his father asked. "I thought we already had a rule about that. You're supposed to shine them twice a week, on Saturdays and Wednesdays. Right?"

"Right, Dad," Harley said.

"Well, when was the last time you shined them?"

Harley tried to remember, but his father didn't wait for an answer. He turned to Davidson.

"And you, your hair is a mess. You'll have to do something about those cowlicks."

"I try, Dad," Davidson said. "I really try to get my hair to stick to my scalp. Yesterday in school I even used paste, but the teacher made me wash it out."

"Harley, I expect you, as the oldest one," his father was saying, "to keep order in this house."

And he folded his paper and left the kitchen.

Harley looked after him for a moment and then angrily began to jam the cereal bowls into the sink. That's how it went most of the time. His father would say that he was the oldest, and he expected him to make his brothers behave, but he would never say anything about respect. And respect was one thing Harley could no longer live without.

He wanted respect like other kids wanted bikes and things like that. He wanted respect most of all from his brothers. He wanted them to respect him when he bossed them around. But they simply ignored him or talked back. Sometimes he was able to scare them by threats of horrible punishments, but his father punished them rarely and never in any horrible way. Most often Harley would have to hit his brothers. But hitting them didn't make them respectful.

He wanted respect from his father too. And his father didn't give it to him. He wanted respect from Mrs.

· II ·

Bruno, the housekeeper. And she didn't give it to him either. Mrs. Bruno came at ten o'clock every morning and left at six. Although she threatened to quit every day, she had stayed longer than any other housekeeper that year. But Mrs. Bruno, like all the other house-keepers, treated Harley as if he were no different from his brothers. The only person who had understood about how it was with Harley had been his mother.

Riding his bike to school, Davidson thought about his problems and how they might change if he had a mother. He was sick and tired of being the peacemaker of the family. It was always he who had to patch up Mott and Harley's quarrels. And what did he get for all his troubles? He got bossed by Harley, he had to play nursemaid to Mott, and his own father didn't appreciate him.

Almost every evening his father yelled at him. That was because while his father was at work Davidson was patient, kind, and nice to everyone. But at the end of the day he was apt to be pretty cranky and mean and lose his temper. But that was because he had been so good all day long.

If he had a mother, she'd be around to see him during those long hours when he was at his best. If he had a mother, she could help him keep peace in the family. She would help him with Mott, who was just a little kid and needed taking care of. And she would yell at Harley whenever he got too bossy. And she would be someone he could talk to. And she would appreciate him—something nobody did, not even his own father.

During recess Mott didn't go out into the school-yard. Ever since breakfast he had been thinking that it would have to be up to him to do something about getting a mother. Now he kept sitting at his desk, look-ing at Miss Lord, his second-grade teacher, and think-ing hard. And getting nowhere.

He had been looking at Miss Lord all morning long, trying to figure out how it would be if she were his mother. For one thing, he was sure she'd give him the best grades. And he hoped that she wouldn't even *let* him do any homework. She'd probably stop yelling at him in front of the class, and she'd quit making him stand in the corner. His life in school would be pretty easy if Miss Lord were his mother. But he wasn't at all sure what she'd be like at home.

"What is it, Mott?" Miss Lord asked him after a while. "Aren't you feeling well? Why aren't you out playing with the others?"

"I'm O.K.," Mott said. "Hey, Miss Lord, are you a good cook? Can you make banana cake and junk like that?"

Miss Lord smiled and Mott wished she hadn't. She had wide spaces between her teeth.

"I guess I am a pretty good cook, but I'm not so very good at baking. Why? Do you have a recipe for banana cake you'd like to share with me?"

"Do you always wear those blouses and skirts?" Mott

asked, without bothering to answer her question.

"What do you mean, dear?"

"I've never seen you wear a real sparkly dress or anything," Mott said. He tried to imagine Miss Lord in something full of jewels and flowers. But he couldn't.

"I guess," Miss Lord said, "I'm just not a very flashy dresser."

It was right then that Mott decided she wouldn't do. He was willing to forgive her for the spaces between her teeth, but he wasn't quite as willing to forgive her for not wanting to wear fancy things.

A few months ago, in a magazine, he had seen a woman who wore a dress that looked like a Christmas tree. If he got a mother, he'd save enough money to buy her a dress like that. And Miss Lord probably wouldn't like it.

He got up from his desk and ran out. There was a girl in first grade he wanted to talk to. Her name was Suzie, and everybody knew that her mother was divorced and then had married again. Suzie was out in the yard, skipping rope. He wanted to ask her how her mother had gotten a new father for her.

"Hey," Mott yelled, pulling Suzie's skirt to get her away from the other girls. "How did your mother get you a new father?"

"Mott Elliott, you leave me alone!" Suzie shouted at him.

"All I wanted to know . . ." he began, but she was already back jumping rope and sticking her tongue out at him.

Mott sat down on the steps of the school building and began to feel very depressed. He had to *do something*! He simply couldn't stand it anymore, not having a mother.

When Mott got home that afternoon, he went to look for Mrs. Bruno. He usually didn't bother talking to her. She was always busy or yelling at them. But today he decided to ask her advice. He found her in the basement, folding the wash.

"Hey," Mott said to her, "where can you see lots of women?"

But Mrs. Bruno wasn't listening to him. She was examining the laundry and muttering to herself about it.

"In the laundromat—" she was saying. Mott bolted out of the basement without waiting to hear the rest. "They sure get clothes cleaner in the laundromat," Mrs. Bruno finished.

Mott got on his bike and pedalled fast to the town's laundromat. He wasn't supposed to go that far, but this was important. If he could find a mother at the laundromat, even Harley wouldn't yell at him for going that far from home. If he found a pretty one, he decided, he'd bring her home right away for his father to see. And if his father liked her, then Harley and Davidson could never again treat him like a little kid.

There were only three women at the laundromat. None of them looked like the kind of mother Mott wanted. One was so fat that her shorts were coming apart at the seams. Another had curlers in her hair

and two black lines instead of eyebrows and a sort of thin moustache over her upper lip. And the third looked at him so angrily that he was afraid she'd hit him if he kept staring at her. But he kept staring, because she did have something he had never seen on a lady—a beautiful black eye.

Mott pedalled home. On the way back he was trying to figure out if it would be all right to write Santa Claus for a mother. He wondered whom he should ask about that. Certainly not Harley or Davidson. They'd only laugh. And his father might yell at him. But if it were all right to ask Santa Claus, how would he describe the kind he wanted?

The woman he liked in the magazine picture, the one wearing a dress like a Christmas tree, was the kind he would like best of all. She had jewels and feathers and bows. She wore all those shiny, bright things not only on her dress but also in her hair and on her face. She actually had jewels glued to her forehead and even to the side of her nose. Her earrings were made out of little bells, and she sparkled and glowed from head to toe.

If he had a mother like that, Mott thought, he could hear her and see her coming from a long way off, and he would always have time to wash up before she got to him. And one of his problems would disappear.

He had all kinds of problems, most of them having to do with being bad. But he just couldn't keep track of all the things that were supposed to be bad. For instance, coming home late was bad only if his father noticed what time it was. If he didn't notice, it wasn't bad at all. And it was bad to bring things to the house. But once he had fished some wet junk out of the river, and his father said it was the prettiest piece of drift-wood he'd ever seen. He hung it up on the wall of his study. After that, Mott brought home anything he saw floating in the river, but he was always yelled at for bringing junk home.

By the time Mott got home, he felt very unhappy. His brothers had already taken their ponies, Spumoni and Tortoni, out of the corral. He guessed they would be riding across Mrs. McCoy's fields by now, but he didn't feel like saddling Pony Baloney all by himself. Recently his pony had gotten into the habit of backing up while being saddled, and no matter how much Mott shouted and yanked, Pony Baloney would move backwards in circles.

The boys were supposed to exercise their ponies each and every day except when it rained or snowed. So Mott climbed up on Pony Baloney's back by holding on to the pony's mane. He was going to ride around the corral bareback. But Pony Baloney didn't feel like it. So Mott sat on the pony for a while, trying to remember where he had put the magazine picture of the lady who looked as pretty as a Christmas tree.

Frog, the sheep dog, came out from his shady hiding place under the cellar door and looked at Pony Baloney and then at Mott.

"I bet you chewed the picture up," Mott yelled at Frog.

Frog, the sheep dog, shook his head against a fly that was trying to land on his nose, and Mott laughed.

"Maybe you didn't," he said. "Maybe it's somewhere in the bedroom. Let's go and find that picture."

He jumped off the pony and didn't even bother to close the corral gate. He was going to look all over his room until he found the magazine. The lady's name might be somewhere under the picture. He could write her a letter and ask her if she wanted to be his mother. Then he could save the money in his piggy bank for something else. She wouldn't need anything since she already had the grandest looking dress in the world and lots of jewels.

The boys' bedroom was a mess. That morning the boys had tried to fly their kites out of the window, and the kite strings were still all over the place.

Mott began to wind up the string that belonged to Harley's kite. He liked it much better than his own, which had a picture of Superman on it. Harley had Batman on his. Davidson's had no picture at all. It was a plain bright red.

Frog, the sheep dog, had followed Mott up the stairs and was now tugging at the kite string. Mott, in trying to get it away from Frog, put his fist right through Batman's face.

"Hey, see what you made me do?" Mott screamed at Frog. He was going to hit Frog, but the sheep dog dove

under the bed. Both he and the cat were used to getting out of the way fast.

Mott slid down the bannister. He went into his father's study, which was out-of-bounds for the boys, and got some paper and glue with which he hoped to fix Harley's kite.

But nothing seemed to go right for Mott that day. No sooner had he brought the glue up to the bedroom than it spilled all over the rug. Mott tried to rub it off with Davidson's pajamas. The top stuck to the bottoms. Then he tried to find a good hiding place for the sticky mess. Finally he stuffed the pajamas behind the radiator, a place which he used for storing all kinds of things that belonged to his brothers and which somehow got broken while he played with them.

The wet glue was still in the middle of the rug, and before Mott could figure out what to do about that, Frog put his nose right into it. Then because the glue was not to his liking, he tried to rub it off and got a piece of Mott's unfinished spelling paper stuck to his nose.

Frog looked so funny Mott couldn't help laughing. He laughed so hard he rolled under Davidson's desk, and when he got up he hit his head on it, and the lamp fell down and broke.

Now the room was a worse mess than ever. Mott got a comic book and put it over the spot where the glue had spilled, and then he tied two of Davidson's socks together and bandaged the lamp.

But Harley's kite still had a hole right through Batman's nose. Mott pushed a chair to the closet and climbed up with the kite. He tried to wedge it into the top of the closet. The kite broke. The thin wooden strips just snapped in his hands. Mott got very mad. He climbed right down from the chair and threw the kite out of the window in disgust. It landed in a tree and looked nice there.

At that very moment Harley happened to be riding back and saw Mott throwing out his kite. He jumped off his pony, Tortoni, without even bothering to put the pony in the corral, and rushed upstairs.

"I saw you! I saw you!" Harley yelled at the top of his voice. His face was very red, and his teeth were making that gritting sound. "I saw you throw my kite out of the window!"

Mott looked up at him in surprise. He had forgotten all about the kite. He had found a tin soldier with a broken head and was trying to fix it by sticking the head on the soldier's bayonet.

"That's mine too!" Harley screeched, yanking the soldier away with one hand and pushing Mott with the

other. Mott fell down and started to yell. That made Harley even madder. They began to hit each other and screamed louder and louder.

Davidson, hearing the racket, got off his pony, Spumoni, and rushed inside the house. He bumped into Mrs. Bruno.

She fell down, spilling the bowl of cake batter she was holding in her hands. Most of the batter landed on Davidson, and he started screaming at her, and Mrs. Bruno was yelling right back at him.

Brat, the cat, left his hiding place under the couch to find a quieter place to hide. Frog, the sheep dog, who had been waiting for days for Brat, the cat, to come out, began to chase him all over the living room.

The ponies, Spumoni, Tortoni, and Baloney, pushed the kitchen screen door open and began to eat some lettuce that was drying in a wire basket over the sink.

Mott and Harley screamed and shouted.

Davidson joined in the fight.

The ponies finished the lettuce and moved over to the apples and pears that were on the kitchen table. Mrs. Bruno saw it all and gave up.

"I've had it," she said. "I quit!"

She jammed her hat on her head, slammed the front door, and was gone.

How it continued...

*T*hey were all gathered around the kitchen table, having one of their "conferences," as their father called these talks. They had one each time a housekeeper quit or after each major fight or crisis in their lives.

"All right," Mr. Elliott was saying as he rapped the table with the spoon. "We've agreed it wasn't anybody's fault. Not even Frog's or Brat's or Spumoni's or Tortoni's or Baloney's."

"Hey, how about Mrs. Bruno? Was it all her fault?" Mott asked.

"No, it wasn't even Mrs. Bruno's fault," Mr. Elliott said. "We've lost her for the same reasons we've lost all of the other housekeepers. We've done things wrong. We must decide what to do now that would be different from what we've done before."

"We could get us a mother!" Mott yelled. "We've never done that!"

"Shut up!" screamed Harley and Davidson together.

Mr. Elliott rapped the table once more.

"We have a rule around here," he said sternly, looking at each boy in turn. "We keep our voices down and we *think*. Right? Harley, do you have any ideas? How are we to cope now?"

Harley cleared his throat. His father had asked his advice. And that was something like being respected.

"I think," Harley said, "that we must get another housekeeper right away."

"Very good," Mr. Elliott said, "except how are we going to keep her this time? Chain her? How are we going to make sure that the housekeeper will stay? Davidson?"

Davidson's hand was up in the air, and now he had a chance to have his say. "We should pay her a lot of money," he said and smiled at his father.

"I don't think," his father said, "that there is enough money in the world for that. We have had six housekeepers in the last few months. Not one of them would have been willing to stay even if I had been able to pay them twice what they were getting. Don't you see? We are in trouble this time. Yes, Mott?"

Mott had been waving his hand for some time. Both Harley and Davidson looked up toward the ceiling, expecting their brother to say something very dumb.

"I think," Mott said, "that the housekeepers we've had were used to girls not boys. They don't know that boys are not as good as girls. Isn't that right, Dad?"

"Do you believe that, Mott?" his father asked. "Do you believe that there are other boys who can't keep from fighting all the time, who *always* get holes in their new pants, who have dirty sticky fingers—*all the time*? Do you know what those housekeepers have to put up with? Don't you understand why they quit? It's a losing game they're playing. The moment they're through cleaning up after you, you arrive to dirty things up. Do you ever put things back in the icebox after a snack? Do you even close the icebox door? Do you go anywhere without leaving a trail behind? Of broken things, of dirty prints? Now, what are the three of you going to do about all that?"

"We're going to change," the three of them said very loudly, and they all meant it this time.

"Do I have your promise?"

"Yes," they all said, and then they came up to their father and shook hands. When they were gone, Mr. Elliott called an employment agency.

"Sorry, sir," the lady who ran the agency said. "We couldn't send anyone to you. The word gets around, you know. I doubt very much that you'll be able to find anyone from these parts willing to work for you."

Mr. Elliott decided to write an ad. When he was through, he telephoned it to *The New York Times*.

"I would like to place an ad under 'Help Wanted,' " Mr. Elliott said into the phone.

"Is it for a domestic?" the lady on the other end of the line asked.

"Yes, it's for a housekeeper."

"I knew it. You sound very harassed," the lady said.

"Oh," sighed Mr. Elliott, "I do already?"

"Yes, sir, you certainly do. Have you made up your ad, or would you like some help?"

"Wanted," Mr. Elliott read from a piece of paper lying on his desk, "a housekeeper. Three boys, motherless home. Good pay."

"May I suggest," the lady from *The New York Times* said, "that you add something to that?"

"Anything you say," Mr. Elliott said and sighed again.

There was a moment's silence on the other end of the line, and then the lady spoke. "How about this? 'Wanted: A housekeeper, must be loving and patient with three motherless boys.' With this type of ad you might get a good woman with a kind heart."

"That's exactly what I need," Mr. Elliott said, thanked her, and hung up.

He felt like crying. Sometimes the job of bringing up his sons seemed too much for him. And sometimes his need for a wife was greater than the boys' for a mother. The need was like a big emptiness in all four of them, and Mr. Elliott was often scared of that emptiness.

Harley had come downstairs after another fight. This time the boys had fought over how good they were going to be once they got a new housekeeper. Now he stood in the door of his father's study feeling very guilty. But not because of Mrs. Bruno or because of the fight. Something that had happened last year made him feel guilty. All he knew right now was that he had to get rid of that feeling of guilt. He had to see and talk to his father.

"Dad," he began, coming into the room. He wasn't quite sure how to go on.

"What can I do for you?" his father asked. "Or should I say what have you done recently? Are the ponies fed? Is your homework done? Are your brothers still alive and well?"

"I want to say . . ." Harley hesitated, and then plunged right in. "I want to say something important to you, Dad."

"Oh." His father smiled up at him. "You have my undivided attention."

Harley shifted his weight from his right foot to his left and looked down at the floor. He knew this wasn't going to be easy.

"Remember about a year ago?" Harley coughed to clear his throat because his voice rose up. "Remember when you were seeing this lady you went to school with, the one I didn't like?"

"I remember," Mr. Elliott said.

"Well . . ." Harley shifted his weight again and looked harder at the floor. "I sort of messed things up for you then, didn't I?"

"You told me you would run away from home if I married her."

Harley had not liked her. She was always going

around saying how cute Mott was and what a darling boy Davidson was, and she hardly ever said anything nice about him.

"Yeah," Harley said. "But it was worse than that. I made Davidson and Mott act like a couple of nuts so that she'd hate all of us . . ." He stopped and waited for his father to say something.

But his father said nothing.

"Well," Harley continued, now speaking very fast. "I'm sorry about that. And I just want you to know that if you ever pick someone else you'd think of marrying, I will try to like her. And even if I don't, it wouldn't matter. Anyone you want to marry would be O.K. with me."

"I'm happy you told me this, Harley," his father said very seriously, although he wanted to smile and hug his son. "If I ever fall in love, I'll let you know."

"Anyone you choose will be all right with me," Harley said, feeling very good now. "She won't even have to understand about me and how tough it is to be the oldest. I was just a kid last year anyway."

"I'm glad you grew up so fast," his father said. "And thanks."

"O.K., Dad." Harley turned on his heels and left his father's study. He felt a lump in his throat as if he had done something extremely fine. Now all he had to do was lay down the law to his brothers.

Each time Harley had a fight with both Davidson and Mott, he knew he would find them together, plotting. They were in the barn, buried in the hay, so that Harley could only see the tops of their heads and an elbow and a shoe, both belonging to Mott.

Ordinarily he would have eavesdropped on them and made fun of their plans for revenge. But today was different. He had to talk to them seriously, and he had to make them listen to him.

"I see you guys," Harley said. It wasn't the very best beginning because both Davidson and Mott got angry.

"We weren't hiding!" Mott shouted down from the hayloft.

"Let's not talk to the creep," said Davidson.

"Yeah," Mott agreed. "Let's never talk to him as long as we live." He rubbed his arm which Harley had twisted during the fight.

"I'm sorry," Harley said. It was the very first time that he had apologized to either of his brothers without being made to.

"Hey, he said he's sorry," Mott whispered loudly to Davidson.

"Dad made him say it," Davidson said, still feeling the pain in his shin where Harley had kicked him.

"Dad didn't make me!" Harley said, climbing up the rope ladder. "I'm sorry on my own."

They didn't try to push him down, for once. And they didn't say anything to make him angry, so he smiled at them and again felt that lump in his throat. He settled himself in the hay, and for a while no one spoke.

It was like that every time they made up after a fight. Always, for a little while, they would feel the warmth for each other. It would only last for as long as no one said anything, but they didn't care how brief the feeling was. They were just glad it was there.

"I've talked to Dad," Harley said after a while. He hoped that this time they would not interrupt him, that they wouldn't start fighting, until he explained things to them. "I've told him that anyone he wants to marry would be O.K. with me."

"Hey, has he got someone? Has he found someone to marry?" Mott asked, surprised.

"No, there is no one," Harley said patiently, but his hand was itching. That meant he really wanted to rap Mott one for interrupting. But he controlled the feeling. "That's what I want to talk to you guys about. I bet the reason he hasn't brought anyone home recently is because of the way we acted last year. We were really mean to . . ."

"Hey, remember how I scared her once?" Mott shouted. "Remember the time I hid under the sofa with my toy mouse?" He and Davidson laughed, and Harley glared at them. "She jumped a foot in the air!" Mott yelled and rolled in the hay with joy at the memory of how scared she was.

"Remember what I did once?" Davidson said. He jumped up and began to limp around, making dreadful noises and terrifying faces. Mott was laughing very hard now and Davidson too. They were both having a great time. "She thought I was a mental retard!" Davidson managed to say between fits of laughter.

"Stop it, you guys!" Harley yelled at them.

But they wouldn't stop. They remembered all the jokes they had played on the woman they had been afraid their father would marry. They remembered all the silly things they had said to her and how one day she rushed out of their house in tears.

"We can never be that bad again!" Harley yelled at them. And then because they would not listen to what he wanted to tell them, he began to hit them. They screamed and shouted so loudly their father heard them all the way from the house.

For punishment Harley was locked in the bedroom. Davidson was sent to the basement. And Mott was taken shopping by his father.

Mr. Elliott hated going to the supermarket. He had always left that job to the housekeeper. The store's bigness and brightness made Mr. Elliott nervous, and his long grocery list frightened him. How was he going to find all the things he needed?

Mott, who trailed behind his father, thought the supermarket was fun. And it seemed to him a perfect place to look for a mother.

The women at the supermarket were all sizes and shapes. Some were pretty, some were ugly; some were fat, some too thin. Some had hair that looked like haystacks, some wore baggy slacks, some wore dresses that were too tight. Some looked cranky, some looked mean, and some looked just so-so. There were not too many Mott liked, and those he did like had kids with them or walked side by side with men. He wanted to find one who was pretty, nicely dressed, and alone.

He finally saw one between the soup cans and the juices. She wore bright-blue shoes, and her high heels went tap-tapping on the linoleum floor. She had on a dress with flowers, and he ran after her to see if she had a pretty face. He pulled at her skirt, and when she looked down, he saw that she wasn't bad to look at. He took her by the hand and dragged her to his father

before she had a chance to know what was happening.

"Hey, what's wrong with this one?" Mott asked his father so loudly that half the people in the supermarket heard him.

Mr. Elliott's face got as red as Harley's did when he got mad. But Mr. Elliott was not mad. He was terribly embarrassed.

"I'm sorry," he said to the lady with blue shoes.

"What was that all about?" the lady asked, but Mott was no longer around. He had spotted a better one.

This one wore a shiny red raincoat, and he was crazy about that. With her head cocked to one side, she was trying to choose between lamb chops and pork chops. She looked a little like a robin, he decided. He liked the way she wrinkled her nose and the way her eyebrows went up towards her brown hair.

Mott's father was at the meat counter by now, so Mott yelled over to him:

"Hey, Dad, what's wrong with this one?" And he pointed to the lady who looked a little bit like a bird.

This time Mr. Elliott grabbed Mott by the hand and pulled him to the very end of the meat counter. The lady in the red raincoat looked after them in surprise.

"Mott, I want you to stop that," Mr. Elliott whispered angrily.

"All I'm trying to do is to . . ." Mott didn't finish the sentence. A fat lady with an overloaded shopping cart came between them and stepped on Mott's toe. He yelled at her: "I wouldn't want you for a mother!" and kicked at her cart.

Then he wandered off because he thought he saw a lady dressed in something that looked almost like a Christmas tree. But he couldn't find her between the aisles of the supermarket and decided he had imagined her. Instead, he found near the bread counter a blonde lady who looked very nice, although her dress was very plain. He took her hand. She peered down at him.

"Are you lost, or am I?" she asked him twice.

Mott didn't answer but kept pulling her to where he had left his father. Mr. Elliott was putting several packages of hot dogs into his shopping cart when Mott appeared with the shortsighted lady by his side.

"Hey, Dad," Mott said, "how would you like a blonde one?"

His father's face looked redder than Harley's ever did. And this time Mott thought that his father even gritted his teeth. Mr. Elliott apologized to the blonde lady. She went off, and he turned to Mott.

"You're going to stay with me from now on," he said, taking hold of his son's hand. He held on tight, and Mott could do nothing but follow wherever his father went.

Mott didn't even bother looking around anymore. He felt very mad. It was no use. He would never understand his father. What was wrong in trying to find a mother? Why was his father angry with him? All Mott had tried to do was find him a wife. He should be glad instead of mad, Mott thought, holding back his tears.

They were in the check-out line right next to a great round pyramid of canned peaches when Mott saw her again, the one he barely had a glimpse of before. She was even prettier than the lady in the magazine. And she did look like a Christmas tree. She was the prettiest lady he had ever seen.

She had on a big blue hat with three roses on the very top of it. Below the hat she had blonde hair, and below the blonde bangs was a pink face with shining blue eyes. She wore a polka-dot dress, gold stockings, and shiny black shoes. There were large earrings in her ears that made a tinkling noise and bracelets on her arms that shone. Everything about her sparkled, including her white teeth when she smiled down at Mott.

Mott was filled with great and sudden happiness. He did not even notice the large sign she held in both her hands. The sign said:

TOO MANY THINGS
YOU DON'T NEED?
GIVE WHAT YOU DON'T WANT
TO THE ANNUAL RUMMAGE SALE

Mott looked at his father, but his father had not seen the beautiful lady. He was staring straight ahead at the line in front of the cash register. He still looked angry.

She might go away, Mott thought desperately. He pulled at his father's sleeve and with the other hand pointed at the lady. He meant to whisper, but his voice rang loud and clear.

"Hey, Dad, there is nothing wrong with this one!"

Mr. Elliott turned to apologize and saw the smiling face of the overdressed lady. He was so surprised and embarrassed that he backed into the canned peaches.

The cans tumbled down. The three of them—Mott, Mr. Elliott, and the lady—were buried under them. But most of the cans landed on the lady.

People screamed and shouted. The supermarket manager came running. His assistant was calling an ambulance. The assistant's assistant was calling a lawyer. The checkers stopped checking. The shoppers stopped shopping.

Everyone was staring at the pile of spilled peach cans.

The first one to come out of the pile was Mott. He wasn't even hurt. He came out laughing. He was laughing because the pretty lady's hat had sailed off her head as she fell and landed on top of his father's head. It was the funniest thing Mott had ever seen—his father getting up with a hat full of flowers on his head.

"Are you all right?" his father asked Mott. Mott looked fine, so he turned to the lady.

"Are you hurt?" he asked and pulled her by the hand.

"Ouch," she said. "Don't pull on that one. I think it's broken." Then she looked up at Mr. Elliott and laughed.

"Why are you laughing?" Mr. Elliott asked, annoyed. But by now everyone who saw him was laughing.

"You're wearing my hat," the pretty lady said and tried hard to stop laughing.

Now the store manager and the assistant manager and the assistant's assistant all crowded around them.

"The ambulance is on its way," one of them said.

"But will you be all right?" Mr. Elliott was worriedly bending over the pretty lady. With her unhurt hand she took her hat off his head and smiled at him.

"I've broken my arm twice before," she said. "Why

don't you call me tomorrow to find out whether I've died or gotten better." She gave him her phone number.

"I'm awfully sorry," Mr. Elliott said. "It was all my fault."

"It was not!" Mott, who had been watching and listening, shouted. "It was my fault!"

He didn't want his father to take credit for what had happened. And what had happened was something very nice. His father and the pretty lady seemed to like each other a lot. He couldn't wait to tell Harley and Davidson about that.

But when he did tell them all about what had happened at the supermarket, instead of being proud of him they both got very mad.

"You're a jerk," Harley said.

"You're a jackass," Davidson added.

"Hey," Mott screamed, surprised. "All I was trying to do was find you a mother!"

"Shut up," yelled Harley.

"Shut up," shouted Davidson.

Mott went upstairs. He felt like crying. He lay down on his bed and closed his eyes against the coming tears. He was never going to try to do anything for them again. He didn't care anymore what became of them. He wasn't ever again going to talk to Harley or Davidson. Not as long as he lived. He would have nothing more to do with them.

Mott turned his face to the wall. When he heard Harley and Davidson coming up the stairs, he wrapped his blanket around his head. He didn't intend to see them or listen to them. All he wanted was for them to leave him alone.

If he had a mother, he wouldn't even sleep in the same room with them. He'd sleep with her. And he wouldn't even play with them. He'd play with her. And he wouldn't even look at them. He'd only look at her. And he'd talk to her about them, and he'd tell her how mean they had always been to him.

And he just might take her away and go somewhere else to live with her. She could ride Tortoni, because Tortoni was almost as big as a horse, and he would ride his own, Pony Baloney. And Spumoni could carry their things on his back. They would go away at night, and they would never come back.

They would find a place somewhere far away, and maybe later, years later, they would send for his dad, and he could bring Frog, the sheep dog, and Brat, the cat. And if they had been very good, Harley and Davidson could come along. But just for a visit, and then they would have to go back.

"We have to have a plan," Harley was saying in a low whisper to Davidson. Mott could hear him through the blanket.

"What kind of a plan?" Davidson whispered back.

"A really good plan for getting us a mother," Harley said. "That stupid jerk Mott doesn't even understand that a mother for us means a wife for Dad. It's got to be someone Dad likes."

"That's right," Davidson said thoughtfully.

Mott was very tempted to stick his head out and yell at them that he understood that. Hadn't he already found a pretty one that his father liked? He had done that all by himself, without any help.

"Dad must like her enough to love her," Harley was saying.

"Yeah, he must like her enough to want to kiss her and junk like that," Davidson agreed.

"And she has to know all sorts of things," Harley said, "like cooking good and sewing patches on our trousers without yelling at us. And she must know the New Math so she can help us with our homework."

That was too much for Mott. He stuck his head from under the blanket and yelled:

"She wouldn't have to know any math!"

"Shut up," they yelled back at him, and he dove under the covers.

He put two fingers in his ears so he could not hear what else they were saying. It didn't matter, anyway, what they said. She wouldn't live with *them*! She would live with *him*!

He wouldn't care if she never cooked, and he wouldn't care if she never sewed. And he certainly wouldn't care if she couldn't add two and two. If she wanted to know that, he could tell her. He was pretty good at math.

And besides, they would probably live on some deserted island. They could eat fruits off the trees and raw fish out of the sea, and she would never have to worry about adding or how to cook. And he would be very careful about his pants. Or better still he could cut them off at the knees.

Mott fell asleep smiling to himself. He dreamt about a beautiful country with low-flying pink clouds and blue water all around. When he looked at the sandy beach, there were women as far as his eye could see, and each was pretty, and all of them were dressed in fancy clothes. And on their heads there were jewels and flowers. And they were singing a song to him. And the song went like this:

> *Mott, we love you.*
> *Truly we do.*
> *We want to take care of you.*
> *Won't you choose one of us*
> *And let the others pass?*
>
> *Choose just one of us.*
> *One is just right*
> *To be your mother*
> *And a wife for your father.*

He could not make up his mind. They were all so pretty. And the longer it took him to decide, the louder they sang. Their arms were waving toward him. He was saying "Eeny-Meeny-Miney-Mo" when the alarm clock rang and woke him up.

How it ended...

Sunday after church Mr. Elliott called the young lady from the supermarket.

"How is your arm?" he asked her.

"It's twice as big as it used to be," the lady said.

"Oh, my goodness," said Mr. Elliott, very worried. "Why is it so big?"

"Because of the cast," she said. Then she laughed, and asked him if he wanted to come to her house and see it.

Before Mr. Elliott left, he warned his sons to behave themselves and not to go outside.

"I am expecting some phone calls," he said. "If anyone calls about the housekeeper's job, I want Harley to take down their numbers. I'll call them back in an hour."

"O.K., Dad," Harley said. Then because his father had made him feel important, he added, "Don't worry about a thing."

"I can't help but worry," Mr. Elliott said and sighed. Each time he left the boys alone he worried. As a matter of fact, that's what he told the young lady when he saw her. And he told her much more, things he had not meant to tell her.

"Sometimes," he said, "it all seems so hopeless. I don't even know if I've done a good job bringing them up."

She listened well and didn't say much until he was ready to go. Then she said, "Even with one arm I'm better than no one. Why don't you let me help you out until you find a housekeeper?"

"I couldn't ask you to do that," Mr. Elliott said.

"But you're not! I'm asking. May I?"

"Would you really?"

"I'd love to," she said and smiled. "I'll come tomorrow afternoon, and by the time you come home from work I'll have dinner ready."

And then they smiled at each other, and each felt happy that they had met.

Meanwhile at their house the boys were talking.

"I wonder what the new housekeeper from the ad will be like," Davidson was saying to Harley.

"She'll be as crummy as all the rest." Harley sighed.

"Hey, I wish we could get a really nice one for a change," Mott said, forgetting that he wasn't going to talk to them as long as he lived.

"Maybe we could," Harley said very slowly. "Maybe we could make sure that she'll be nice."

"How?" Davidson and Mott asked.

Harley thought before he spoke.

"We could," he finally said, "talk to the housekeepers ourselves. We could tell anyone who calls to come tomorrow after school, before Dad gets back from work."

"What good would that do?" Davidson wanted to know.

"Hey, that's no idea," sneered Mott.

"Listen, you stupids!" Harley yelled at them. "I haven't finished!" Before they could say anything, he continued fast, trying not to let his anger get the better of him. "We could make a sort of a test for the housekeepers. If one of them answers all the questions right, she can have the job."

"That's a good idea," Davidson admitted.

"Hey, let me make up some questions," Mott screamed, but right then the phone rang.

Harley told the caller to be sure to come on Monday afternoon after three and then hung up. But the phone rang again and twice more before they could start making out the test.

While Harley was on the phone both Davidson and Mott tried to think of what kind of questions the test should have. They used up a lot of their father's stationery in trying. The wastepaper basket was full of discarded pieces of paper before Harley joined them.

"Here." Davidson handed Harley a whole bunch of his father's stationery, which they were not allowed to use. "You're the oldest, so why don't you try to make up the questions."

"Besides," Mott said, "it was your idea in the first place."

"We have to think about this together," Harley said. "Now, what kind of a housekeeper would you like?" He had asked Davidson, but it was Mott who answered.

"Someone who wouldn't mind me yelling," he yelled.

"He asked me," Davidson said, pushing Mott. Mott pushed Davidson, and there would have been another fight, but Harley shouted to them to stop.

"We've got work to do," Harley said. "O.K., Davidson, how about you? What do you say?"

Davidson thought for a while and then said that he would like to have a housekeeper who'd appreciate the fact that he was good most of the day.

"How about you?" Davidson asked Harley. "What kind would you like?"

"Someone who'd respect me because I'm the oldest," Harley said.

But saying what they had said did not help them with the questions they wanted to ask.

"This is all wrong," Harley decided. "We should make sure that whoever we get doesn't mind us being bad—because we are bad."

"Yeah, I guess we are," Davidson agreed.

"Maybe we are," Mott admitted. "But then let's just tell them we are before they find out for themselves." He thought for a moment and then yelled, "How about this for the first question: 'Do you like to yell?' If they don't like to yell, they wouldn't do it so much."

It took half an hour before they made the list of questions they intended to ask, and by the time it was finished the list looked like this:

Do you like to yell?	Yes____ No____
Do loud noises make you nervous?	Yes____ No____
Do you hate taking care of animals like ponies?	Yes____ No____
Do you think boys can be as good as girls?	Yes____ No____
Do you think spoiling kids is bad?	Yes____ No____
Do you mind if we forget sometimes to be good?	Yes____ No____

Harley read the list aloud.

"The great thing about this," he explained, "is that we'll only hire the one who answers No to every single one of these questions."

They all examined the list again, and sure enough the perfect housekeeper would be the one who would answer No again and again.

"That's really neat," Davidson said. And they all

shook hands and told each other that they were great. And once again they were filled with love for each other, the feeling making each one happy and proud. And this time it stayed with them a little longer, almost for ten minutes. And then they had a fight.

"Hey," Mott yelled, "we could use a list like that to get us a mother."

Neither Harley nor Davidson thought this right, and they began to argue among themselves. Harley swung at Mott, and Davidson swung at Mott, but Mott ducked and they hit each other.

By the time their father returned, they were fighting with pillows. Feathers were flying all over the place.

The fight accomplished at least one thing. Their father was too busy yelling at them to see his spoiled stationery or ask if anyone had called in answer to the ad.

The next day they hurried back from school. They straightened up their room and even dusted the living room a little bit and made the kitchen fairly clean. They didn't want to give a bad impression of their home to the housekeepers.

The first to arrive was a fat lady whose name was Mrs. Kellogg. They liked her fine, especially her booming laugh. She shook all over when she laughed, and she laughed a lot. But when they gave her the questions, she answered Yes to two of them, about loud noises and taking care of the ponies.

"We have to try to find someone who'd say No to

each and every one of the questions," Harley explained to her. "But if we can't find someone like that we'll call you."

"That will be fine," she said, and laughed and gave them her phone number. "Imagine three little kids interviewing for a job," she was saying as she went out of the house.

"She was nice," Davidson said.

"Hey, she liked me," Mott said.

"I liked her too," Harley said. "But let's wait and see if we can do better."

The bell rang again, and when they opened the door, there were not one but two ladies. Twins. They looked exactly alike and dressed alike and spoke alike. But they were both nervous and didn't laugh even once. And each had four Yes answers.

Harley thanked them and said they wouldn't do. They were quite put out and left the house, looking mad.

The next applicant was very tall and kept her nose so high in the air that they were sure she could not see anything in front of her. She wouldn't even take the test.

"Is there a cook?" she asked. "And a maid? Do you have a chauffeur?"

When they laughed at her questions, she stormed out, saying she'd never been so insulted in all her life.

"Maybe," Davidson said, "we should call Mrs. Kellogg. She was really nice."

"We shouldn't have asked her about the ponies,"

Harley said. "It's our job to take care of them anyway."

"Yeah," Davidson agreed.

"Hey, if we call Mrs. Kellogg," Mott yelled, "we can tell her we'll be quiet so she won't be nervous about the noise."

"Yeah, fat chance of that with your big mouth," Harley said, and Davidson laughed.

They would probably have had another fight if the front doorbell hadn't rung at that very moment.

Mott, who was the only one who had seen her before, didn't recognize her. Instead of flowers and bows, dots and gold stockings, sparkly things and noisy jewelry, she wore a very simple blue dress. Her left arm was in a sling, but not even that made Mott think of the overdressed lady from the supermarket.

Each of them thought her awfully pretty, and Harley handed her the paper with the questions.

"The one about the ponies," he told her, "you don't have to bother about."

Mott wanted so badly for her to pass the test that he yelled: "Hey, you should answer . . ." But Davidson put his hand on Mott's mouth and kicked him.

They bent over her, watching her read the list. Her eyes were smiling at them when she looked up.

"That test is too easy," she said. "The only right answer to all of these questions is No. Even the one about the ponies. Do I win or lose?"

"You win!" the three of them shouted.

"What do I win?" she wanted to know.

"You can have the job," Harley told her. "It's all yours. When can you start?"

"Today!" Mott yelled. "And you can live in the bedroom downstairs. Please stay with us!"

He was tugging at her skirt, and Davidson slapped his hand away.

"You were the only one," he explained to her, "who answered everything right."

"Can you live with us?" Mott asked. "You must come and live with us." He climbed on a chair to be nearer to her. But he didn't hear her answer. Harley pulled him down.

"I'm sorry," Harley said. "He's just a little kid and acts like a pest most of the time."

"But he doesn't mean to be a jackass," Davidson added, glaring at his younger brother.

But Mott didn't sulk. He smiled his widest smile at her.

She had guessed what it was all about. Their father had expected housekeepers to apply for the job. She didn't know if she should tell them that she had not come for that. What harm would it be, she thought, if I played the game? Or maybe even took the job?

"I can cook pretty well," she said, "but I can't sew. And the worst thing of all is that I can't clean. My mother always said that I was neat but dirty so . . ."

"That's O.K.," Harley said before his brothers could say anything at all. "We could work it out. If you keep things neat, we'll keep them clean. O.K., you guys?"

"Sure," Davidson and Mott yelled at the same time.

"And I can teach you how to be clean," Mott added.

She laughed because his face was very dirty, and there was a chocolate-milk spot on his shirt. But his brothers didn't laugh. They hit him instead.

Harley hit Mott on the head, and Davidson hit him on the back. And Mott yelled. Then they yelled back at him not to yell in front of her. And she got a little scared because they yelled very loud, all three of them. They were in fact yelling so loudly that they didn't hear her say:

"Please don't yell."

She said it once. Then she said it again.

"Please don't yell."

And after she said it the third time and they were still yelling, she walked to the door.

"Where are you going?" they yelled after her.

She put her good hand to her ear, and they didn't know what was the matter with her.

"Are you sick?" Harley asked.

"Do you have an earache?" Davidson wanted to know.

"Hey, do you want an aspirin?" Mott screamed, very worried.

"I guess I was wrong," she said when they quieted down and were listening to her.

"About what?" Harley asked.

"On that question about the noise. I should have said Yes to that one. I just can't stand as much noise as you can make."

"But you're hired," Harley shouted.

"You can't go," Davidson screamed.

But Mott didn't say anything at all. He went up to her and took her by the hand. He just held on to her, and she bent down to him because he was whispering something that she couldn't make out.

"What did you say?" she asked.

"I won't scream again," Mott said.

He said it so low that neither Harley nor Davidson heard him. He himself could barely hear his own words. It was strange and new, not hearing himself shout.

"If you stay, I won't scream again," he promised, and again his voice was too low to be heard by his brothers.

"All right," she said. "I'll stay."

"Hey, that's great!"

It was no use. Mott had shouted again. I've got to watch it, he reminded himself. I've got to watch it all the time.

"Do you want to see the downstairs bedroom?" Davidson asked.

"Yes, let's see your room," Mott said, not too loud.

"She doesn't want to see the dumb bedroom," Harley said angrily. He was mad at them for having suggested what he himself had wanted to suggest. And he was angry at Mott's still holding on to her hand. "Let me show you our ponies," he said and pulled her away from Mott.

"Come and see our room instead," Mott said.

"No, come with me," Davidson said, pushing both of them away.

She felt frightened again. This time they weren't shouting, but they wanted her to go to three different places at once, and she didn't know how she could do that.

They were pushing and pulling at her.

"Listen," she said and shook their hands off. "I won't push you around if you don't push me around. And let's have one rule: We'll either do things together or in turns."

"That's all right with me," Harley said. "I'm the oldest, so my turn comes first."

"Not necessarily," she said. "That could lead to fights."

"Well, how are we going to work it out?" Harley asked, feeling a little sad. But he wasn't going to get mad at her, he decided. Not unless she gave him a good reason to get mad.

"This time let's start from the top," she said.

"Our bedroom is at the top of the house," Mott said.

"All right then," she said. "Let's start from there and go through the whole house."

They watched themselves pretty well. Only a few times an argument started, but it got nowhere. She saw to that. She had trouble keeping from feeling flattered by their attention and knew that would be her problem. She understood better that each of them had a problem too. Harley was too bossy, Davidson too impatient, and Mott too loud. But they all tried, as best as they could, to behave themselves.

Mott tried the hardest and the most often. Each time he spoke—and he talked more often than his brothers—he used a lower voice, until by late afternoon he was quite hoarse from speaking softly so much.

When they heard their father's car in the driveway, they asked her not to tell him that they had hired her for a housekeeper.

"What will I tell him then?" she wanted to know.

"That you'll stay because you're our friend," Harley said.

"That way he won't yell at us," Davidson added.

"Hey, we've got to go ride our ponies now," Mott said. He didn't want to be around just in case their father decided to yell at them anyway. He didn't want to be yelled at in front of her.

As they saddled their ponies, they were hoping things would go right between her and their father. And Davidson and Harley spoke about that.

"Maybe Dad will like her a whole lot," Davidson said.

"Maybe he'll like her so much," Harley said, "that he would rather have her for a wife."

Mott didn't dare hope aloud. Instead, he said, "Let's take a real long ride."

That way, he thought, his father would get to know her well, if they were gone for a long time. And then he decided something: If she became their mother, he would not take her away. They'd all stay together in the house.

As they rode their ponies each thought of how it

would be if she stayed on not as their housekeeper but as their mother.

Harley knew that he could talk with her. She had a lot of common sense. She would know without being told about how it was with him—how he hated to act mean, how he needed respect. He could stay up later than Davidson and Mott, and when his brothers were asleep in bed, he would talk to her. Sometimes they'd talk through the whole night. He would like to learn all about her, and he would teach her about himself and his brothers. He would even tell her that their father had his troubles too. For one thing, he wasn't very good at getting his way. She could help him with that. Both of them could work together at keeping peace in the family, and then Davidson wouldn't have to worry so much.

Davidson was thinking how she would probably hide the shedding flowers. She said she was neat but dirty, so she would know how to do that without having to clean all the time. And he was sure she already knew that Mott was just a baby and had to be looked after. The two of them could be patient with him—and with Harley. He hoped she understood that he was the one she could depend on to keep his brothers from acting too wild.

And Mott was making plans how he could pretend all sorts of things so that she would pay more attention to him than to anyone. He could pretend to be sick, and he could even paint spots on his face. If she thought he had measles, she might even let him spend the night in her bed. He decided that with her he would not mind even if she kissed Harley and Davidson once in a while. That would be all right with him. Even if she kissed his father all the time, he wouldn't mind.

And just as he was thinking that, Mott realized who she was.

He was about to yell to his brothers that if it hadn't been for him, they'd never have met her. But he stopped himself just in time. It would be better, he thought, if it were a secret—just between him and his father and her. And if sometime they decided to tell how they first met, then Davidson and Harley could come to him and thank him. He could wait.

When the boys returned home later that evening, it was almost dark. They put their ponies in the corral and walked into the house very quietly. They didn't actually mean to spy. They just wanted to see how she was getting along with their father.

The two of them were in the kitchen. She was trying to toss the salad with one hand. Mr. Elliott was helping her, and they were laughing about something. The boys didn't stay around to find out what they were laughing about. They crept up to their bedroom.

"You know what?" Harley said.

"What?" Davidson and Mott asked.

"We ought to let them eat dinner alone."

"Hey, how come?" Mott asked. He had planned to sit next to her.

"It's a good idea," Davidson said. "If they ate alone, they'd get to know each other better."

"Oh," said Mott and sighed.

"Let's clean up this mess," said Harley. "Now I want this room to look shipshape. If we keep it clean, she can keep it neat, and that way it will look just fine."

After cleaning up for a while, Mott said that he had to go to the bathroom and as long as he had to do that why couldn't he go downstairs and tell her and their father that they were letting them eat dinner alone?

"We should tell them together, all three of us," Harley said.

"We'll all go down in a little while," said Davidson. "You just go to the bathroom and come right back."

But the temptation was too much for Mott. He just had to see her again. He slid down the bannister. He was trying to listen to what they were saying in the kitchen, but he couldn't hear a thing.

"Are you spying on us?" It was his father, and Mott was ready to bolt upstairs before he was yelled at. But his father didn't yell at all. He was smiling up at Mott.

"You know, Mott," his father said, "for once in your life you were right."

"About what, Dad?" Mott asked, surprised.

His father came closer to the bannister. *cop 3*

"You were right," his father whispered, "when you said at the supermarket that there was nothing wrong with this one." And with his finger he pointed towards the kitchen, and then he laughed.

Mott ran upstairs. He opened the door of the bed-room. It seemed awfully nice and bright and clean inside their room. And both Harley and Davidson were standing in front of the mirror slicking down their hair. And they had clean shirts on.

Mott rushed to his own closet and pulled out his Sunday suit. If they are getting ready, he thought, to have a mother, I better get ready too.